CW00848337

The Weenies of the Wood: LOST IN THE SNOW

Written & Illustrated by E M Wilkie

Copyright © 2015

www.aletheiabooks.co

Winter has come, and in the pine wood,
under the branches of the tall trees,
there is a lovely blanket of white snow.

You can see animals in the forest.
And, if you look very carefully,
you might see tiny windows in the tree trunks.
You might even see the Weenies of the wood!

Grandpa and Grandma Weenie are visiting Tree Trunk Cottage. Through the upstairs window, you can see Daddy and Mummy Weenie, and the children: Teeny Weenie, Bitty Weenie, and Wee Weenie, the baby.

Teeny and Bitty Weenie are getting ready to go to school.
They are very excited because it's snowing!
"Don't stray from the path!" warns Daddy.
"You might get lost in the snow!"

**Mummy and Wee Weenie wave
Teeny and Bitty off to school.
"The snow is beautiful!" says Teeny.
"I wish we didn't have to go to school!" says Bitty.**

It stops snowing and Teeny and Bitty
explore the wood.
Everything looks so different in the snow!

"Let's build a snowman!" says Bitty.
They begin to gather snow. It's great fun!
Soon they forget all about going to school.

"Let's build an igloo," says Teeny.
"I don't think it's as good as the Eskimos'!"
says Bitty.

"Let's have a snowball fight!" suggests Bitty.
Teeny is very good at throwing snowballs.
One knocks Bitty right over in the snow!

"I'm cold," says Bitty.
"Which way is school?" asks Teeny.
The wood looks the same in every direction.
They don't know which way to go!

It begins to snow again.
"We're lost!" says Bitty.
"We left the path," adds Teeny. "Daddy told us to
stay on the path so we wouldn't get lost!"

They take shelter under some bushes. They are very cold and hungry. They wish they were at home and safe inside Tree Trunk Cottage.

"I hope Daddy will come and find us," says Bitty.

The snow gets heavier and heavier.
Teeny and Bitty feel very lost and alone.
They wonder whether they
will ever be found.

They wait a long time. At last they hear someone
shout, "Teeny? Bitty? Where are you?"
"It's Daddy! And Grandpa too!" cries Bitty.
"They've found us!" shouts Teeny.
"Daddy! Grandpa! We're over here!"

**They are very glad to be rescued by
Daddy and Grandpa Weenie.
"We're sorry we left the path," says Teeny.
"We're sorry we didn't go to school," says Bitty.**

"Never mind that just now," says Daddy.
"We'll have you home in no time," adds Grandpa.
They begin to walk home.

The snow is very deep.

It seems like a long, long way home.

When they are too tired to walk any further,
Daddy and Grandpa carry them.

**At last they reach Tree Trunk Cottage.
Mummy and Grandma Weenie are waiting
for them at the door.**

Soon they are warm and safe and snug.
Mummy makes lots of lovely things for tea!

Grandpa sits in the big armchair and reads to them from the Bible.

"The Bible says we are all lost," says Grandpa.
"But we're not lost now!" say Teeny and Bitty.
"You and Daddy came to find us!"

"That's not what I mean," says Grandpa. "We are all lost because we have done wrong things. The wrong things take us away from God— away from the right path."

"How do we get back to God and onto the right path again?" ask Teeny and Bitty. "Who can find us like you and Daddy found us when we were lost in the snow?"

"God's Son, the Lord Jesus, came to find us and save us," says Grandpa. "If we trust in Him, He makes us right and keeps us on the right path. We are never lost from God again!"

The next day Teeny and Bitty went straight to school. They never forgot the lessons they learned about being lost!

For more adventures of

THE WEENIES OF THE WOOD

see

www.aletheiabooks.co

"For the Son of Man has come to seek and to save that which was lost."

Luke 19:10, The Bible

13572244R00018

Printed in Great Britain
by Amazon.co.uk, Ltd.,
Marston Gate.